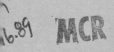

An I Can Read Book™

Harry's Pony

by Barbara Ann Porte
pictures by Yossi Abolafia

HarperCollins*Publishers*

Watercolor paints and a black pen
were used for the full-color art.

HarperCollins®, 🍎®, and I Can Read Book® are
trademarks of HarperCollins Publishers Inc.

Harry's Pony

Text copyright © 1997 by Barbara Ann Porte
Illustrations copyright © 1997 by Yossi Abolafia
Printed in the U.S.A. All rights reserved.
www.harperchildrens.com

Library of Congress Cataloging-in-Publication Data
Porte, Barbara Ann.
Harry's pony / by Barbara Ann Porte ; pictures by Yossi Abolafia.
   p.   cm.
"Greenwillow Books."
Summary: When Harry wins a pony in a contest, his friends try to find
a way to help him keep it, but it is his aunt and her friends who come up
with a solution.
   ISBN 0-06-050657-1 — ISBN 0-06-050658-X (lib. bdg.) —
ISBN 0-06-050659-8 (pbk.)
   [1. Contests—Fiction. 2. Horses—Fiction.] I. Abolafia, Yossi, ill.
II. Title.
PZ7.P7995Haqq   1997   96-43675
[E]—dc20   CIP
                                         AC

1 2 3 4 5 6 7 8 9 10
❖
First HarperCollins edition, 2003
Originally published by Greenwillow Books,
an imprint of HarperCollins Publishers, in 1997.

For Deborah and Russell
—B. A. P.

For Avi
—Y. A.

I, Harry, am the owner of a pony.

I won it in a contest:

In fifty words or less

tell how you like Jam Pops.

Send five box tops

and ten side labels

with each entry.

This is what I wrote:

I, Harry, love jam pops.
So does my pop.
Pop pops his in the toaster.
I dip mine in fried eggs—
only the yolks.
I call it dipsy doodle.
"Don't forget to brush
your teeth,"
pop says when we finish.
He is a dentist.
I don't have cavities yet.

"Yippee!" I shout.

"I won a contest."

Pop pokes out his head.

"What's all the commotion about?"

he asks. I show him my letter.

"Dear Harry Moskowitz:

Congratulations!

Your entry has won first place

in the Jam Pops contest.

First prize is a pony.

Please call 1-800-123-4567

to arrange for delivery. . . ."

In small type at the bottom it reads:

"Winner may elect to receive
a bicycle instead."

"Congratulations," says Pop.

"There's nothing like a new bicycle."

"Thank you," I say.

"But if it's all the same to you,

I'd rather have the pony.

I already have a bike."

"*Mazel tov*," says Pop,

which means good luck.

"Now you'll have two."

I was afraid that he would say that.

"Please please please," I beg him.

"I've always wanted a pony."

My father sighs. "Harry, believe me.

A pony in this house isn't possible."

"Well, of course not," I say.

"It wouldn't stay in the house.

Ponies like living outside."

"Sure, outside in the country,"

says my father.

"We live in the suburbs.

There are zoning regulations.

'No ponies,' they say."

Then he goes back inside.

Later Aunt Rose stops by to visit.

I show her my letter.

"Congratulations, Harry," she says.

"I always wanted a pony."

My father clears his throat.

"Well, a bike is nice, too," she adds.

That's when I get an idea.

"Could my pony live with you?"

I ask her.

"It would keep Girl company."

Girl is my dog who lives

with my Aunt Rose

because my father is allergic.

Aunt Rose smiles but shakes her head.

"I'm sorry, Harry," she says.

"A dog is one thing.

A pony's something else altogether.

Besides, there are

zoning regulations."

At school the next day

I discuss it with Dorcas and Eddie.

I explain about zoning regulations.

"Maybe they only mean

permanent ponies,"

Eddie says after a while.

"What if yours was just visiting?"

"Visiting?" I ask.

"Sure," says Eddie.

"It could visit you, then visit me,

then visit Dorcas—then begin again."

"That's a great idea," says Dorcas.

15

After school they ask their parents.

"Absolutely not,"
Eddie's mom tells him.

"No, no, no,"  says Dorcas's dad.

But Sylvia, Dorcas's older sister,
tells Dorcas, "If I won a pony,
I'd go into business."

"Business?" I say the next day

when Dorcas tells me.

"Sure. Sylvia says the regulations

probably apply only to pet ponies,

not working ones. Sylvia says

the first thing you need to do

is get a business license.

"Eddie and I can be your partners.

We'll put up signs."

"We can take pictures
and sell them," Eddie says.
"Parents love pictures
of their children on ponies."

"Wearing cowboy hats," I say.

"I can rent them mine."

I have a cowboy hat collection
from my last birthday party.

"When we earn enough money,
we'll buy a cart," says Dorcas.
"Then we can do birthday parties.
We'll get rich."

After dinner and the evening news,

I tell Pop our plan.

"The money I earn,

I'll put into a savings account

for college," I promise.

My father sighs.

"Harry, have you any idea

what it costs to keep a pony?"

he asks.

"A pony eats more than just grass.

You need to buy it hay and oats

and vitamins;

also blankets and brushes,

a saddle and a bridle.

If a pony gets sick,

you may need to call a veterinarian.

Veterinarians are expensive.

Even a healthy pony needs shots.

Every few months it needs shoeing."

Pop stops talking to catch his breath.

Just as I'm wondering

how he knows so much about ponies,

he adds, "Believe me, Harry,

you'd get rich much quicker

by selling one of your bicycles."

Well, sure, I think.

But then what would happen

to my pony?

"My father said no," I tell Dorcas
and Eddie in school the next day.
"Maybe I should run away,
with Girl and my pony."
"You mean *ride* away, don't you?"
asks Dorcas.

"Where would you go?" asks Eddie.

That's when it comes to me.

"To Oklahoma, to live with

my Grandma and Grandpa Murray

on their peanut farm," I say.

"My mom had a horse

when she was my age."

We look up Oklahoma

on the map.

"It looks very far.

What if you got lost?" says Eddie.

"What if you got arrested?"

asks Dorcas. "I think pony riding

is not allowed on highways.

"You'd have to wait in jail

until your father came to get you.

Who knows what would happen

to your pony? How awful!"

A tear comes into my eye.

I try not to blink.

I don't want anyone to think

I am crying.

After school I hurry to Aunt Rose's.

Friday is my day

to take Girl for her walk.

Aunt Rose's band is there.

They've been rehearsing.

Now they're packing up

their instruments.

"Hi, Harry," some say.

"Congratulations," say others.

"*Mazel tov,*" says Herbert,

the French horn player.

"It's not every day

a boy wins a pony."

"Or a bicycle," adds Lucille,

the drummer.

"See you tomorrow,"

they say as they leave.

Except Wild Mamie,

the clarinet player, doesn't leave.

Neither, of course,

do Aunt Rose or Uncle Leo.

"Cheer up, Harry.

You're looking awfully glum

for someone who's just

won a contest," Uncle Leo says.

"Have a cookie," says Aunt Rose.

"Wild Mamie was just telling us

about a pony farm."

"A pony farm?" I say.

"The Red Barn Pony Farm,"

says Wild Mamie.

"I'm a volunteer there.

"Before my accident

I rode wild horses in rodeos.

That's how I got my name.

Now I teach

children with disabilities

how to ride ponies

and take care of them.

They could really use

your pony on the farm."

I'm surprised to hear all this,

especially about Wild Mamie's name.

I always thought it came from

how she drove her wheelchair.

She takes out pictures

of the farm to show me.

I look at them carefully.

The children all look happy.

So do the ponies.

"Of course, it's up to you,"

Wild Mamie says.

"But I think you couldn't find

a better home for your pony."

I look at the pictures some more.

"You don't have to decide

this minute," says Aunt Rose.

"Take your time," Uncle Leo says.

"Talk it over with your father."

"Right," says Wild Mamie.

"Think about it.

Then, if you decide to give

the farm your pony, let me know.

I'll make the arrangements."

"Yes, I will," I say.

Then I get Girl's leash
and take Girl for a walk.
"At least I'd know where my pony is
and that it has a good home,"
I tell her.
"Plus it would have
other ponies for company."

At dinner I discuss it with Pop.

"I'm sure it would be good

for the farm and the pony,

but a new bicycle is nice, too.

It's up to you," he tells me.

Later, in bed, I think about it,

trying to decide.

That night I dream

that I'm a cowboy,

riding a bicycle in a rodeo.

I'm trying to rope a pony

in a wheelchair.

Each time I almost do,

my bicycle falls over.

39

I wake up in the morning

on the floor.

While brushing my teeth,
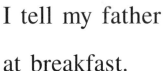

I think about my pony some more.

"I've decided to give my pony

to the farm,"

I tell my father

at breakfast.

"Are you sure?" he asks me.

"Yes," I say. "Then at least

I'll know where my pony is

and that it has a good home.

I don't need another bicycle."

I telephone Wild Mamie to tell her.

Then she talks to Pop.

She calls me back that night.

"Everything is set," she tells me.

"I've talked with the people

at Jam Pops, and also at the farm.

The pony will be delivered next week.

Red Barn would like you there

on Friday to make the presentation."

"I think you made

a good decision,"

Pop tells me.

I hope he is right.

I think it's too late now

to change my mind.

Friday, the day of the presentation,

Pop picks me up early from school.

Aunt Rose and Uncle Leo are with him.

I change my clothes in the car.

I put on my cowboy boots

and my blue cowboy hat.

I tie it under my chin.

I hope there won't be too much wind.

When we arrive at the farm,

my pony is there.

So is Wild Mamie.

She gives me a carrot.

"Hold your hand flat

and keep it still," she tells me.

That's what I do.

My pony eats the carrot.

Then it nibbles my hat.

I think it likes me.

Soon a limousine arrives.

A person from Jam Pops gets out.

Pop and I sign some papers

that show the pony's all mine.

A newspaper reporter and

a photographer are also there.

They take pictures and ask questions.

I explain to them

about zoning regulations.

"Anyway, a farm's much better

than a yard for a pony," I say.

Then it's time for the presentation.

I hold on to my pony's reins.

The head of Red Barn leans on her cane

and makes a short speech.

"On behalf of the children,

their parents, and the Red Barn staff,

I thank you," she says finally.

"You come back anytime now

and visit," she adds.

"Thank you. I will," I tell her.

Then I hand my pony's reins
to a tiny girl named Cindy
who is standing next to me.
She hands me a trophy.
It is a statue of a pony.

Just then a breeze blows by.

My hat comes untied.

I reach up and catch it.

Everyone claps.

"Thank you," I say.

All the way home in the car

I hold my trophy in my lap.

Harry Moskowitz

Friend of

the Red Barn Pony Farm

is engraved on the base.

I put it in my room

beside my hat collection.

The next day there is

a picture in the newspaper

of Cindy, me, and the pony.

I cut it out and paste it

in our family album.

Who knows? I tell myself.

Next contest I'm in, maybe I'll win

a pair of Rollerblades.

That would be much easier.

Later I ride my bicycle

to Aunt Rose's.

Girl is in the yard.

I tell her all about the presentation.

"It turned out fine," I say.

"Red Barn Farm has a new pony.

The pony has a good home.

I have a trophy, and

my hat didn't blow away."

Girl barks as if

she's glad to hear it.

"What's all that commotion about?"

Aunt Rose asks, coming to the door.

"Oh, it's you, Harry.

Come on in. I've just baked

oatmeal cookies."

I follow her in to have some.

Girl wags her tail

and comes with me.